DEXTER'S LABORATORY™

I DREAM OF DEXTER

BY Pam Pollack and Meg Belviso

Based on "DEXTER'S LABORATORY," as created by Genndy Tartakovsky

SCHOLASTIC INC.

New York   Toronto   London   Auckland   Sydney
Mexico City   New Delhi   Hong Kong   Buenos Aires

ISBN 0-439-43423-8

Cover and interior illustrations by John Kurtz
Designed by Maria Stasavage

12 11 10 9 8 7 6 5 4 3 2 1   3 4 5 6 7 8/0

Printed in the U.S.A.
First printing, February 2003

Chapter 1

Dexter, boy genius, paced nervously backstage. He waited for his name to be called. His palms were sweating. He was really nervous. But who wouldn't be? It's not every elementary school student who wins the Nobel Prize in Physics, Chemistry, Mathematics, Biology, and Starship Maneuvers all at the same time. Finally, he heard the announcement.

"My esteemed Science colleagues," the man onstage said into a microphone. "You are the smartest, most intelligent, brainiest scientists the world has ever known. Now put your hands together for the scientist we wish we all could be. The kid who put the *pro* in *proton* . . . Dexter, boy genius!"

Dexter hurried out onto the stage. He walked up to the microphone and shuffled the note cards he'd carefully prepared. He was ready to make his acceptance speech. As he opened his mouth he heard a giggle from the audience. Then he felt a breeze someplace he was not expecting it. Slowly, Dexter looked down at himself.

"Great Einstein's ghost!" he exclaimed. "I am in my underwear!"

The auditorium erupted with laughter. The scientists laughed so hard they burst the buttons on their lab coats. Their pens fell out of their pocket protectors. Their glasses fogged over.

Dexter tried to hide behind the microphone, but it was impossible. Then one laugh cut through all the others, like nails scraping on a blackboard: HA ha. HA ha. HA ha HA ha HA ha.

"Mandark!" Dexter hissed, searching the crowd. Sure enough, there he was. Dexter's archenemy. His black hair was like a bowl on his head. A white streak ran around it like a lightning bolt. His big black glasses jiggled on his nose as he laughed. Mandark. The evil boy scientist who wanted to destroy Dexter's lab. This couldn't be happening. It had to be . . . a nightmare!

Dexter sat up straight in bed. His heart was beating fast. His pajamas were tangled up in a knot and his pillow was over one foot. "What a horrible dream," he muttered. He looked at the clock. He couldn't see it without his glasses, but it was still dark outside. "Plenty of time for more sleepy sleepy."

Dexter fixed his pillow and his pajamas, rolled over, and fell back to sleep.

This time, he dreamed he was discovering a formula for a genetically engineered cold cereal that would never go soggy in milk. But just as he held up his test tube in triumph, a voice behind him yelled, "Eureka! I, Mandark, evil boy genius, have developed this formula a mere second before Dexter finished his!"

Dexter turned around to face Mandark. "Nooooo!" he cried.

The scene changed. Now Dexter was sinking to the

DROWNATOPIA
MANDARKANSAS

bottom of the ocean in a nuclear-powered submarine, searching for the lost city of Drownatopia. When he touched down, Mandark was already waiting for him. He'd renamed Drownatopia "Mandarkansas."

"Noooooo!" cried Dexter.

The scene changed. Mandark's robot army creamed Dexter's robot army. Mandark's lab rats ran circles around Dexter's lab rats. Mandark won first place in the state science fair. Dexter got a ribbon "for trying so hard."

"Nooo!" cried Dexter. "No! No! NOOOO!"

Dexter sat up in bed. His head was down where his belly should be. His pajamas were on backward. His pillow was on the ceiling. His alarm clock was ringing. It was time to get up.

"These nightmares could not have come from my own beloved brain," Dexter said. "Clearly, Mandark, my archenemy, has developed some kind of REM Invading Vibrational Ray. Now he is using it to invade my personal dreamscape. The fiend! He must be stopped or I will never sleep again!"

Chapter 2

Dexter immediately drew up plans for a Psionic Dream Protector Helmet to keep Mandark out of his dreams. He wanted to start work on it right away, but before he could go into his lab —

"Hi, Dexter!" His sister, Dee Dee, danced into the room, her ponytails bouncing. "It's time for breakfast," she sang. "It's time for school. I love ponies, they're so

cool!" Dee Dee danced out of the room again, then stuck her head back in. "Mom says come down right away. We're having waffles," she said. Then she disappeared.

If it weren't for the waffles, Dexter would have gone straight to his lab. But it was waffles, so he went downstairs.

"Morning, son," his dad said. Mom put a stack of waffles on his plate and poured the syrup so it made a smiley face on them. "You look like you didn't get much sleep."

Dexter nodded.

"Neither did I," said Dad. "Darn cats outside were howling all night. Nooooo," Dad wailed, imitating the cats he had heard. "Maaaandaaarkaaaansaaaaas!"

"Heh heh heh," Dexter laughed nervously. He could feel his face turning red. He knew he must create his Psionic Dream Protector Helmet as soon as possible. "Bad kitties," Dexter said. "They will not trouble you again."

Dexter couldn't wait for school to be over so he could get home and work on his Dream Helmet. At the end of his day, he stood at his locker and packed up his books. "I won't see you in my dreams again, Mandark," he muttered. "Not after my invention is complete."

Dexter slammed his locker door to reveal Mandark standing behind it.

Mandark laughed his evil laugh. "HA ha. HA ha. HA ha HA ha HA ha! My REM Invading Vibrational Ray was a complete

success. Now I will control your dreams forever! Foolish Dexter. To think you can foil the dark plans of Mandark, evil boy genius! Your puny brain could never hope to challenge mine!"

Dexter faced his enemy calmly. "Mandark," he said. "Your evil schemes are doomed to fail. Science — beautiful Sci-

ence — will never be bent to your twisted will. I, Dexter, will defeat you!"

Mandark sneered. "I saw you in your underwear in your dream," he reminded Dexter. "You have a freckle on your knee."

Then Mandark skipped off down the hall, laughing, "HA ha. HA ha. HA ha HA ha HA ha!"

"Curse you, Mandark!" Dexter yelled. He did have a freckle on his knee.

Dexter didn't even stop for a snack when he got home. "I made jelly tots!" Mom called after him as he ran up the stairs.

Dexter ran back down the stairs and took three jelly tots and a glass of milk.

"Have fun!" Mom said as he hurried back up the stairs to his room and slipped

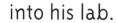

into his lab.

Dexter pulled out what looked like a satellite dish and covered it with aluminum foil and cybernetic transmitters. He attached it to a bicycle helmet that he had magnetized and ionized according to his own alpha pi brain waves. Dexter's alpha pi brain waves were so strong he could do calculus in his sleep. "But not with Mandark lurking in my dreams," Dexter muttered.

Dexter fitted the helmet over his head, adjusted the chin strap for comfort, and switched it on via remote control. Immediately the helmet began buzzing with a

low hum. "It's like my own lullaby of Science." Dexter sighed. "Mandark's REM Invading Vibrational Ray has no chance of getting through my Psionic Dream Protector Helmet."

Dexter's eyes started to close as he listened to the humming and he jerked himself awake. "I have much homework to do before sleeping, my little helmet," he cooed, taking off his new invention. He laid it lovingly on the counter. "Until tonight."

Dexter went down to the kitchen for more jelly tots.

Chapter 3

Meanwhile, several blocks away, in another top secret laboratory, Mandark sat and plotted. He knew his sworn rival very well. Dexter would right now be working on a defense against his REM Invading Vibrational Ray.

"Now what would I do if I were only half as smart as I am now?" Mandark asked himself. He thought he was giving

Dexter credit by saying his rival was even half as smart as himself. Once he figured out what Dexter was up to, Mandark was sure he could come up with something even sneakier. Mandark paced back and forth and tried to think like Dexter, but that made him think of . . .

"Dee Dee," Mandark sighed. "How could such a vision of loveliness be related to my sworn enemy?" Quickly, he did the math. "The chances of it are 5,068,289,586,209 to one!" Mandark picked up the framed picture of Dee Dee that sat right beside his test tubes. "One day, my love, everyone will know that

I, Mandark, am the greatest scientific mind the world has ever known. NOT DEXTER!!"

Back at Dexter's house, another boy genius had already finished his home-work. "So simple!" He had plenty of time before bed to tinker with his Psionic Dream Protector Helmet. After painting it silver with orange stars, Dexter adjusted the ratio of magnetized transmitters to ionized receivers. Now the helmet should give him only delightful dreams. "All I have to do is adjust the antennae and . . ."

"Knock, knock!" Dee Dee called as she skipped past security into his secret lab. "Hi, Dexter!"

Dexter jumped, accidentally bending one of the antennae into an L. "Dee Dee, get out!" he wailed.

Dee Dee did not get out. She pulled something fluffy from behind her back. "Look!" she said.

Dexter examined the thing in her hand. It could be a horse, but it was an unnatural color — peppermint pink. It had a very large head that was mostly big eyes with long, curling lashes. Its mane and tail looked like cotton candy. "Why have you brought this girlish nonsense into a place of Science?" he asked, holding it by the tip of its pink tail.

"It's my new Pony Puff Pony with adjustable eyelashes and press-on hooves!" Dee Dee exclaimed, taking the pony back. She held it above her head and pirouetted. "Her name is Wishing Star and she's the Princess of Pony Land! Tomorrow

night all the ponies are going to her wedding to Prince Prancelot!"

"Dee Dee, I don't have time for pastel animal weddings in make-believe kingdoms," Dexter said. "I am doing Science. If I do not finish my invention by bedtime my archenemy, Mandark, will continue to invade my dreams until I am so tired I am

no longer able to op-
pose his dark plans for
destroying my lab!"

Dee Dee blinked twice,
slowly. Then she pulled out another pink Pony Puff Pony thing.
"Do you want to see her wedding sad-
dle?" she asked.

While Dexter struggled with big sisters
and pony princesses, Mandark was hard
at work. "HA ha. HA ha. HA ha HA ha HA
ha!" he cackled, holding up his latest
invention. "By now, Dexter must have
completed his Psionic Dream Protector
Helmet," he said. "But I, Mandark, have
just completed my Anti-Psionic Laser
Gun. With this invention I can easily break
through Dexter's scientifically inferior

helmet and torment him in his dreams once more. Thank you, Dark Forces! You never let me down!"

Just as Mandark was painting a big M in red nail polish on his Anti-Psionic Laser Gun, the door to his lab slammed open. Mandark turned around in horror. It was his sister Olga, who preferred to be called Lalavava — and you'd better call her that if you knew what was good for you.

"Mandark!" Lalavava yelled. "Where's my red nail polish?"

"Here it is!" Mandark squeaked, running over to his sister. She was so short she only came up to his knees. "You don't even need to hit me!" Mandark handed her the nail polish with his eyes closed. "Please, oh, please, don't hurt me!"

Mandark kept his eyes shut until Lalavava was gone. Then he shook his fist at the sky. "All hail Mandark, the dark genius!" he cried. "Sing a song of Mandark, the greatest genius the world has ever known. NOT DEXTER!"

Chapter 4

Dexter had never been more excited about going to sleep than he was that night. "There is no way Mandark is getting into my dreams. Let him try his best." Dexter slipped on his Psionic Dream Protector Helmet, flipped the on switch, and smiled. Then he climbed into bed and turned off the light.

It was hard to sleep in a helmet. The

chin strap tickled, the satellite dish was heavy, and the antennae kept getting tangled in the Super Galileo Heliocentric Universe Mobile that hung over his bed. He lay there in the dark, listening to his family going to bed.

"Mom," he heard Dee Dee call. "Can I braid Princess Wishing Star's mane before bed? She wants to try out different hairstyles for her wedding."

"All right, dear," Mom said sweetly. "I was the same way before I married your father."

Dexter turned up the buzzing on his Psionic Dream Protector Helmet to drown out the pony talk, and closed his eyes. In moments, he found himself walking through a field of flowers. He knew it was

a dream because he wasn't sneezing, like he usually did when he got near fields or flowers. Dexter looked around him and didn't see Mandark anywhere. "Thank you, little helmet," he sighed. "You have done your job well."

Dexter picked some flowers and continued through the field. As far as the eye could see — no Mandark.

Finally, Dexter came upon a little cottage. He knocked at the door. A man an-

swered. It was Albert Einstein, Dexter's favorite scientist. Dexter handed him the flowers. "For you, sir," he said shyly.

"Dexter!" said Einstein. "We've been waiting for you!"

Einstein seemed to be having a party. All the most famous scientists in history were invited. Dexter greeted them all. "Hey, Pythagoras," he said. "Wonderful theorem!" "Hi, Dr. Celsius. Excellent thermometer. First rate." "Well, hello there, Dr. Schrödinger — where's your cat?"

Einstein stood up on a chair and put on

his glasses to read his latest scientific proof. "And now," the famous genius said, "one hundred reasons why Dexter is the greatest scientist ever. By Albert Einstein. Reason one . . ."

Before Dr. Einstein could get to reason one, the cottage door banged open. There was a puff of smoke. The room went dark. There stood Dexter's archenemy. "HA ha. HA ha. HA ha HA ha HA ha!"

"Mandark!" Dexter growled. "How dare you interrupt all these famous —"

But when Dexter turned back to the party, all the famous scientists were gone. Well, not gone, exactly. They were all still there, but they'd been turned into ducks. Every one of them was waddling around the room, quacking.

"Curse you, Mandark!" Dexter said. "You and your dark, twisted Science. You will never prevail!"

"Aha, but I already have!" cried Mandark. "My Anti-Psionic Laser has broken through your puny Psionic field. I stand here to challenge you. There can be only one boy genius in this town!"

Dexter narrowed his eyes. He pulled out his number two pencil. "So be it!" Dexter cried.

Just as Dexter and Mandark were about to rush at each other there was a terrible noise. Two terrible noises. One was an electronic beep: "BEEP beep. BEEP beep. BEEP beep BEEP beep BEEP beep," just like Mandark would sound if he were an alarm clock. The other was Dexter's own alarm clock. It was time for both boys to get up for school.

Mandark disappeared before his eyes. Dexter woke up in his own bed. He took off his Psionic Dream Protector Helmet. "You win this time, Mandark," Dexter said through gritted teeth. "But tonight, victory shall be mine!"

Chapter 5

Dexter was very tired as he waited for the school bus. "Wake up, Dexter!" Dee Dee yelled every time he fell against her knee.

"What?" Dexter mumbled, adjusting his glasses. "Just resting my eyes."

Finally, the bus rumbled up and the doors opened. Dee Dee skipped to the back where her friends Mee Mee and Lee

Lee were sitting. Dexter made it halfway down the aisle and collapsed into the laps of two kindergartners, flattening them against the seat. When he finally awoke they were at school. "Heh heh heh," he said as he got up. "Was this seat taken?"

Dexter stumbled quickly off the bus and hurried to his locker. He just had time

to find his history book before Mandark appeared at his side. "HA ha. HA ha," he began, but he was too tired to finish. There were dark circles under his eyes, making him look like he was wearing two pairs of glasses.

"Mandark, you fiend," Dexter muttered.

"How's Einstein?" Mandark sneered. "Is he still your *dream man*?"

"Your evil dream ray is no help to you now that we are awake," Dexter said. "Defend yourself and your midlevel IQ!"

Mandark's eyes blazed. He balled his hands into fists. Just then —

"Hi, Dexter!" Dee Dee's voice pierced through the hallway as she bounced up to Dexter's locker.

At the sight of Dee Dee, Mandark's knees trembled. He was so busy watching Dee Dee's ponytails sway back and forth as she bounced off down the hallway, he didn't notice Dexter as he slipped away.

Once he was in class, Dexter started to get sleepy again. His teacher, Mr. Luzinsky, was telling the students about the

Revolutionary War. "It was at the Battle of Bunker Hill," he said, "where the rebel colonel Prescott told his men: 'Don't fire until you see the whites of their eyes!'"

Dexter couldn't see the whites of anyone's eyes. He had fallen asleep. On the other side of the room, Mandark was also beginning to nod off. He had just enough strength to reach into his pocket and pull out his miniature REM Invading Vibrational Ray and flip the switch before closing his eyes.

Dexter dreamed he was a drummer boy at the Battle of Bunker Hill. He could see the British forces in their red coats coming at them. Beside him, Colonel Prescott was tongue-tied. "Okay, men," said Colonel

Prescott. "Don't fire until you . . . hear the rumble of their stomachs! No. Don't fire until you smell the bacon on their breath! No. Until you feel their boots on your toes! No. Darn it! What am I trying to say here?"

Drummer Boy Dexter leaped to his feet. "Don't fire until you see the whites of their eyes!"

"Yes!" cried the colonel. "That's what I meant. To battle!"

The British Army surged up the hill, led by Mandark playing a bugle. "So we meet again, Dexter!" he said, brandishing a musket in the air.

Dexter leaped straight up and hovered as the musket passed below him. Then he did a double flip and landed behind

Mandark. "Welcome to *my* dream!" said Dexter.

Mandark threw away his musket and pulled out a tiny metal box that quickly grew into a robot spider two stories high. Both the American and British armies scattered in terror. Dexter took a metal box from his own pocket. It grew into a robot dinosaur three stories high. They advanced on each other. Mandark's spider wrapped a leg around Dexter's di-

nosaur and pulled him to the ground. Dexter's dinosaur slapped the spider with his tail, sending him rolling down Bunker Hill.

Just then a school bell rang, waking Dexter and Mandark. They both fell out of their chairs and onto the floor. Their teacher glared at them as the other kids headed out for recess. "Naptime is over," Mr. Luzinsky said ominously.

Chapter 6

Mr. Luzinsky gave Mandark and Dexter detention after school for falling asleep during his history lesson. "No visits to Grandpa for me today," Dexter grumbled as he took his seat in the detention room. Dexter was planning to use his detention time to figure out exactly how to combat Mandark's Anti-Psionic Laser, as well as how to get more jelly volume into the

perimeter of the average jelly tot, but Mr. Luzinsky had other plans. He took them down to the cafeteria and handed them both a mop.

"The janitor is out sick," he explained. "We need this floor cleaned up by the end of the day. Get scrubbing."

Mr. Luzinsky disappeared through the

swinging cafeteria doors. Dexter and Mandark eyed each other over their mops. Slowly, they looked at the cleaning fluids they were supposed to use. "Octyl decyl dimethyl ammonium chloride," Dexter read off the label of one bottle. "Might be effective."

Mandark immediately checked the bottle of cleaning fluid he was using to see if it was better than Dexter's. "Alkyl dimethyl benzyl ammonium chloride," he read. "Your puny SparkleForce is nothing compared to the mighty cleaning power of my OutSpotOut!"

Dexter held his bottle of SparkleForce over his head menacingly. "May the best chloride win!"

Dexter and Mandark got to work clean-

ing opposite sides of the cafeteria. "My octyl decyl dimethyl ammonium chloride is doing quite well," Dexter muttered to himself. "But it could use a little help."

Dexter slipped behind the lunch counter and opened the supply closet. There were bottles of soaps, oven cleaners, and drain uncloggers. Dexter got to work reading all the labels. "Nonionic surfactants, boric acid, sodium hypochlorite . . . yes, these will do quite well!" Dexter began mixing chemicals together just like he was in his lab at home.

Little did he know that Mandark had gone into the janitor's closet and was making up his own concoction with the products he found in there. "Anionic surfactants, choloric acid, helium introglodyte . . . yes, these will do quite well!"

Mandark and Dexter both returned to the cafeteria with buckets full of their new Extra Anti-Scummifying Fluids. Slopping their mops into their buckets, they took off across the floor like Zamboni machines.

"HA ha!" cried Mandark. "Your floor will never be as clean as mine!"

"Your floor will never be clean," said Dexter. "Not while you are standing on it!"

When they'd mopped the whole floor, both boys dropped to their knees with sponges. "Must get cleaner," Dexter muttered. "Must beat Mandark."

Mandark scrubbed harder. "Must beat Dexter," he said. "Must get cleaner."

Finally, both boys collapsed, exhausted. Then they sat up and looked at the cafeteria floor. The glare from the shine hurt their eyes. Then they heard a hissing sound. The linoleum started to smoke and pop. The plastic squares curled up and turned black. Dexter and Mandark ran for the hallway just in time to see the entire cafeteria floor evaporate.

They peered down to where the floor used to be and saw only Mr. Luzinsky standing in the teacher's lounge below, looking up at them. Dexter could see the whites of his eyes. And his tonsils, because he was screaming.

"Look what your inferior cleaning formula did," Mandark said.

Dexter gripped his sponge until his knuckles turned white.

"Tonight we shall see," Dexter whispered, "which of us will be mopped up."

Chapter 7

When Dexter came home from school, he locked himself in his lab. He paced back and forth, trying to think of a way to beat Mandark at his own game. He wrote pages of formulas until all of his pencils broke. He programmed his computer to zap him awake every time he fell asleep. "Just resting my eyes," he mumbled when the computer woke him up for the fifth

time. The computer zapped him again just to be sure. "Stupid computer," Dexter muttered.

Dexter completed his latest invention just in time for dinner. He tried to cry out in triumph, but he was too tired, so he just said, "I'm finished." But there was one thing missing. Dexter shuddered to think of the final element in his plan to get Mandark. It was risky, but sometimes you had to work with unstable compounds to get the results you wanted.

"Tonight, Mandark will feel the fury of Dexter unbound," he cried, feeling his energy return. "He will face my REM Assaulting Ray with Ultra-Red Nightmare-Seeking Capability and my most danger-ous secret weapon . . . DEE DEE!"

Thunder crashed outside the lab. The computer zapped Dexter. "Bad computer!" Dexter said. "I wasn't even sleeping!"

At dinner, Dee Dee talked about Princess Wishing Star's Pony Puff wedding. She'd decided on a chocolate wedding cake with grass clippings for the horses. "Grandpa gave me a whole bag of grass clippings. It's going to be a dream wedding!"

"Grandpa missed you today, Dexter," Mom said sadly. "All afternoon he kept asking, 'Where's little Billy?'"

Billy was what Grandpa always called Dexter.

Dexter sighed. He could not think about Grandpa now. Right after dinner he had to go where no scientist had ever gone before. He had to go to . . . Dee Dee's room. Once dinner was over, Dexter forced himself to take the long walk down the hall.

"Come in!" Dee Dee sang when Dexter knocked. Slowly, Dexter opened the door. Bright pink assaulted his eyes. Everything was fluffy. Except the stuff that was frilly. Dee Dee sat on her bed with a copy of *Eleventeen* magazine. "Hi, Dexter!" she said. "Do you want me to do your hair?"

"No, thank you," Dexter said, trying to

48

smile. "Dee Dee, I must ask you . . . I was wondering if you would . . . For the good of Science it is imperative that you . . ."

"That I what?" asked Dee Dee.

Dexter took a deep breath and uttered the eight words he thought he would never, ever say. "Dee Dee, would you . . . come into my lab, please?"

"Sure, little brother!" Dee Dee yelled.

"This better work," Dexter muttered under his breath. "Curse you, Mandark."

When she got into the lab, Dee Dee went straight to the REM Assaulting Ray with Ultra-Red Nightmare-Seeking Capability. "What's this do?" she asked, pressing the big red button on the side.

Dexter didn't have to tell Dee Dee what the REM Ray did because it just did what it was supposed to do. He and Dee Dee were now standing in a room at the top of a tall, dark tower. Lightning flashed outside. The stone walls inside were painted deep red. On one of them hung a portrait of Dexter with a big X through his face.

"Where are we?" Dee Dee shivered.

"Welcome to Mandark's head," said Dexter. "We are in his dream. You will never find a more wretched hive of bad Science and villainy. We must be cautious."

Dee Dee looked around. It didn't look anything like her dreams. There wasn't even a single bunny rabbit.

"Dee Dee, I have brought you here because I, Dexter, boy genius, need your help. If you do this for me . . ." Dexter swallowed and forced the words out. "I promise to make your fondest dream come true."

"Sure, little brother," Dee Dee said.

"What kind of help?"

Dexter pointed to another portrait. This one was of Dee Dee. And it was in a heart-shaped frame. Dee Dee bent down so that Dexter could lift up her ponytail and whisper his brilliant plan in her ear.

Meanwhile, Mandark was dreaming. In his dream he was running up the stairs of his dark tower. He couldn't wait to start doing nasty things to Dexter. He burst into the room, kissed the portrait of Dee Dee, and went straight to the telescope. "Let's see what's going on in Dexter's dream." He laughed. "Probably something not as smart as mine."

Mandark bent down toward his telescope. Before he could focus he heard a sound.

"Tra-la-la," someone sang. "Tra-la-la."

"Who's that?" Mandark whispered. "Could it be?"

Mandark turned around slowly. Dee Dee danced out from the shadows on tiptoe. "*The Dance of the Unicorn,*" she announced. "Act I: A Unicolt Is Born."

Dee Dee tossed her head and pawed gracefully at the ground. Mandark couldn't take his eyes off her. This was just what Dexter had counted on.

And where was Dexter? He was running through the dark halls of Mandark's dream with his Ultra-Red Nightmare-Seeking Ray. He found dozens of Mandark-shaped doors

that led into dark rooms. "Where are you hiding?" Dexter called. "Come to Dexter!" As he got closer to a door with a laser force field protecting it, his Ray started blinking bright red. The sign on the door said NOTHING IN HERE but Dexter's Ray told him differently. "Aha!" whispered Dexter. "This is the room where Mandark has locked his nightmares." Dexter quickly deactivated the force field with a piece of chewing gum and a paper clip. Then he threw the door wide open.

At first all he heard was heavy breathing. Then a battle drum started beating somewhere inside. Dexter heard shrieks and moans in the darkness. Then all of Mandark's nightmares ran out. Bullies from school rushed by, then a giantess who looked like Lalavava, then a dozen Dexters of all shapes and sizes. "Good, my friends," Dexter told them all. "Go find Mandark. You have work to do."

Dexter was about to follow them when he felt hot breath on his neck. He turned around slowly and found himself facing . . . no, it couldn't be. "You are not real," Dexter whispered, backing

away. "I am not afraid of you anymore."

But there, towering over him, just like in all of his nightmares when he was little, was Mr. Soap, whose picture used to be on Dexter's baby shampoo. "TIME TO TAKE BATH!" Mr. Soap roared.

Dexter dropped his Ray and cowered in the shadows. "No wash hair," he whimpered. "Bad Mr.Soap!"

Dexter could hear the squish of the bubble feet coming closer. In another minute he'd be swallowed up by Mr. Soap, just as he'd always feared. Mandark's mother must have used the same baby shampoo. Dexter clutched the only thing he had left, his last number two pencil. "Farewell, beloved Science!" Dexter cried as Mr. Soap pounced on him.

There was a loud *splat*, and Mr. Soap was gone. Dexter's pencil was covered in soapsuds. "That was close," Dexter said. "Now it's Mandark's turn!"

Dee Dee was in the middle of Act II: A Horn Grows in Brooklyn when Dexter burst through the door. Mandark was surrounded by the nightmares that Dexter had unleashed from their prison. The giant Lalavava was dangling him by the collar of his shirt as the twelve Dexters danced

around him and sang, "We're smarter than you are, we're smarter than you are."

"Blast you, Dexter!" Mandark wailed. "To the end of the universe!"

Dee Dee shook her finger at Mandark. "That wasn't very nice," she scolded. "Just for that, you're not invited to the wedding in Pony Land."

"Dee Dee," Dexter said with a smile, "our work here is done."

"Dee Dee, come back!" Mandark cried. "My love!" But Dee Dee and Dexter had disappeared.

Chapter 9

"Dee Dee," said Dexter when they were back home in his lab. "You have helped make my dream of getting even with Mandark come true. And a scientist always keeps his word." Dexter lifted the Dream Ray. "Tonight you shall have the best dream Science can provide."

"Can I dream about anything I want?" asked Dee Dee.

"Anything," promised Dexter, pointing the Ray at Dee Dee. "But please don't dream about —"

Moments later, in Pony Land, Dee Dee rode down Lollipop Lane on a fat little white pony wearing big black glasses and flowers in his curly red mane. "Hurry, Dexter," Dee Dee said, "we can't be late for the wedding!"

"I don't see why I have to be the pony in this dream," Dexter muttered, flicking his tail. "Can't I be the famous scientist

who taught the groom physics when he was just a colt?"

Dee Dee shook her head. They got to the wedding in plenty of time to see Princess Wishing Star trot down the aisle. Dee Dee cried. The bridesmaids nickered. Prince Prancelot smashed a glass with his hoof for good luck. Dexter went over to the wedding cake and feasted on chocolate and grass clippings. It wasn't half bad. He looked around at Dee Dee's dream. It was silly and pink and unscientific. But it was totally Mandark-free.

Tomorrow he would return to his lab, but tonight he would sleep. Beautiful sleep. Science had done it again.

THE END